Happy Hallow

LOVE,

Mrs. Aguilera

A First-Start® Easy Reader

This easy reader contains only 39 different words,
repeated often to help the young reader develop
word recognition and interest in reading.

Basic word list for *Trick or Treat Halloween*

it	here	almost
is	want	Halloween
fun	wants	anything
on	this	Pat
you	busy	Bob
can	she	Mary
be	looks	Jeff
to	like	getting
for	ding	ready
a	dong	clown
he	trick	monster
or	treat	witch
do	what	ghost

Trick or Treat Halloween

Written by Sharon Peters

Illustrated by Susan T. Hall

Troll Associates

10   9   8   7   6   5   4   3

It is almost Halloween.

Halloween is almost here!

Halloween is fun.

On Halloween, you can be anything.

On Halloween, you can be
anything you want to be.

This is Pat.

Pat is busy.

She is getting ready for Halloween.

Pat wants to be a clown.

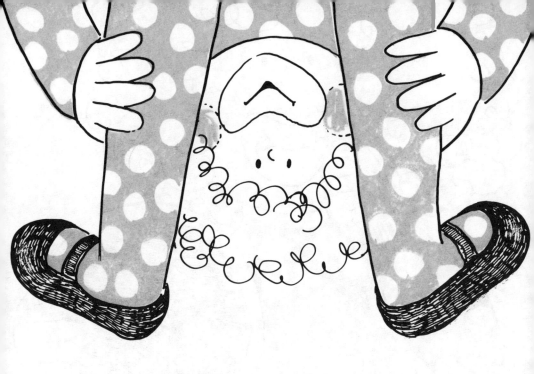

A clown looks like this.

This is Bob.

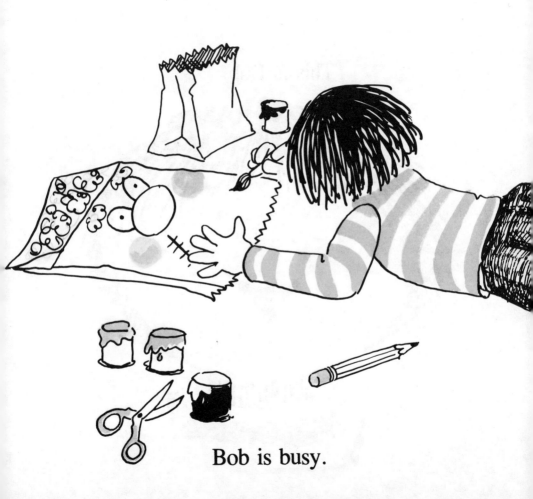

Bob is busy.

He is getting ready for Halloween.

Bob wants to be a monster.

A monster looks like this.

This is Mary.

Mary is busy.

She is getting ready for Halloween.

Mary wants to be a witch.

A witch looks like this.

This is Jeff.

Jeff is busy.

He is getting ready for Halloween.

Jeff wants to be a ghost.

A ghost looks like this.

Ding-dong.
Trick or Treat!

What do *you* want
to be on Halloween?